THE SILVER PONY

HOLLY WEBB

Illustrations by

JAMES BROWN

LITTLE TIGER

LONDON

The leaves started rustling and Daisy felt the
little dachshund beside her give a grateful sigh.
A breeze, at last! It was so hot, even in the
shade under the trees. Betsy had been slumped
on the cool tiles of the kitchen floor, panting,
when Daisy and the others got in from school.
Daisy had thought it might be too hot for
the tiny dog to want a walk in the woods. But
when Daisy had picked up her lead, she had
wriggled to her feet, tail wagging.

"You knew it would be cooler out here,
didn't you?" Daisy murmured, stroking Betsy's

hot little head. "You're a clever girl. Want some water?" She'd put a bottle of water and a plastic bowl in her backpack – her phone was in there too. Mum and Dad didn't mind her taking Betsy for walks on her own, as long as she always took her phone and stuck to the part of the forest she knew. They were lucky to live somewhere so wild and Daisy loved it. She had moved to the New Forest with her parents and her little sister and brother a year before, from a big town.

Dad had been offered a new job and her parents had wanted them to have a chance to grow up somewhere greener. It still felt so special, being surrounded by trees and shy deer and the wild ponies. And now they had Betsy too – she was one of the best things about their move. Although she only ever took Betsy through the woods and out on to the heath as far as a tiny stream, about half a mile from her house, it was far enough to feel like a proper walk.

"It's still too hot, even out here," Daisy muttered. She and Betsy were sitting on the brownish grass, leaning against a fallen tree. Daisy had changed into shorts after school – her summer dress felt too sticky to wear a minute longer. Now she could feel dust and bits of bark clinging to her legs. Usually it was nicely damp under the trees, but today the thick cushions of velvet-green moss on the dead wood felt dry and bristly.

She poured some water from the bottle into Betsy's bowl and the dachshund lapped at it lazily. Daisy drank some too, and then sighed and poured a bit of it over her head.

It dribbled down between her dark curls and she shivered deliciously.

"It should be the holidays," she said to Betsy. "How can they make us go to school when it's this hot? There's a whole week left of term. It's torture."

No one had been running around at break or lunch today. Instead everyone had flopped in the shade, moaning about how hot they were. Luckily it was Friday. No more sitting in the classroom, trying not to fall asleep in the heat, at least not for a couple of days. Daisy leaned back against the tree trunk again and yawned. "We should head back soon," she said. "Otherwise I might go to sleep right here."

Betsy yawned too and snuggled her chin in to Daisy's leg. Her fur was silken, but so hot that Daisy wriggled. "Oof, do you have to, Bets?"

But the little dog stayed squidged up against her. "I love you, but you're roasting… Oh well, go on then. I'll see if Mum will let me get the paddling pool out later on," Daisy suggested. "I bet you'd like that. You'll have to share it with Oscar and Chloe, though. They'll splash. Actually that sounds pretty good right now."

Oscar was seven and Chloe was three – she was at nursery. She loved her little sister but Chloe always wanted her to play and it could be a bit much. Going for walks with Betsy was a good way to escape from endlessly being made to draw mermaids or mix what Chloe called 'science experiments', which basically meant stirring everything her sister could find in the garden up in a bucket.

"I wish Mara would come back," Daisy muttered to Betsy. "It's not the same at school without her." Mara was Daisy's best friend, but she'd gone into hospital during the Easter holidays and Daisy didn't know when she'd be back at school again.

The little dog gave a small half-snore and Daisy sighed. "Yeah, I know. It's boring when I moan. Let's head back. Sorry, Bets. I know it's mean now you're falling asleep. But this was supposed to be a quick walk before dinner. I promised Mum. I hope she's making something cold. Come on…" She tickled Betsy under her chin, and the dachshund opened one eye and glared at her reproachfully.

"Time to go. I know, it's not fair." Daisy jiggled her leg to make Betsy move. "Aw, Bets… I can't carry you home. It would be like carrying a hot-water bottle." But Betsy stayed glued to her leg. "Oh, all right! I'll do it. Just for you. Little monster. Come on then." She scooped Betsy up in her arms and started to trudge back through the trees.

Betsy wriggled and scrambled until she had her front paws resting on Daisy's shoulder and her nose tucked up under Daisy's hair. "Even your nose is hot," Daisy complained, squinting down at her. Then she frowned. She'd thought Betsy was being lazy but maybe she really was suffering. "And it's so dry. Dogs' noses are supposed to be damp, aren't they? Maybe I shouldn't have brought you out."

She started to walk a little faster, wanting to get Betsy home and show her to Mum. When she and Betsy had set off earlier, it hadn't felt like they'd gone far – just down the path that ran into the woods a couple of houses up from theirs. But now, hurrying back, it seemed so

much further. Although Betsy was tiny, she
seemed to be getting heavier with every step.

At last Daisy came out on to the pavement
and she darted up the path at the side of the
house to the back door. Betsy was still slumped
against her shoulder but her tail thudded
gently against Daisy's arm as they burst into
the kitchen.

"Daisy! Are you OK?" Mum said in surprise.

"I'm fine but I think I let Betsy get too hot.
Her nose is dry and she wouldn't walk back.
I had to carry her." Daisy picked Betsy up off
her shoulder and held her out. The little dog
sagged, like she was a limp old beanie toy.
"Oh, Betsy!" Daisy gulped. "I'm sorry, Mum.
I took water with me and she wanted to go
out, honestly she did."

Mum cuddled Betsy close, eyeing the tiny

dog worriedly. "It's OK, sweetheart, it's not your fault. I should have thought about it and said no. But I didn't think it would be too hot for her in the woods. Here, run a dishcloth under the cold tap for me."

Daisy soaked the cloth and then laid it across Betsy's glossy black fur. The dachshund peered curiously over Mum's shoulder to see what was happening.

"Is that nice?" Daisy asked.

"What are you doing?" Oscar demanded, coming into the kitchen to throw his lolly stick in the bin.

"Oh! Do you think Betsy would like a lolly?" Daisy asked, glancing at the freezer.

"You can't give our lollies to the dog!" Oscar sounded horrified. "We need those!"

"So does Betsy. She's really hot!"

"I'm not sure the sugar would be good for her," Daisy's mum murmured. "She's perking up a bit though, Daisy, look. Wet the cloth again for her. Oscar, if you don't want me to feed Betsy a lolly, you can run upstairs and get an old towel out of the cupboard on the landing for her instead."

"Why?"

"So we can wet it for her to lie on," Mum said patiently. "We need to cool her down."

Oscar finally looked at Betsy properly. She was still lying limply in Mum's arms and her eyes were sunken. "I'll get it," he said, racing out of the kitchen. He came back a minute later with a soaking-wet towel – which had obviously just dripped all the way down the stairs. "I wetted it for you in the bath," he explained helpfully.

"Oh… Good." Mum sighed. "Wring it out in the sink a bit. Then we'll put it down under the table where no one's going to trip over her."

Oscar squeezed some water out of the towel and then laid it on the floor under the kitchen table. Betsy peered curiously at it as Mum knelt down. When she was placed on the towel, her eyes widened for a moment and then she stretched out, wriggling a little, as if to let the cool water soak into her fur.

"She can have a lolly if she wants one," Oscar said, watching her. "She looks so hot."

"I really don't think it would be good for her. It might make her sick. Remember when she stole that slice of Daisy's birthday cake a couple of weeks ago? She was sick everywhere."

"Ice cubes! We could give her an ice cube!" Daisy suggested. "Please, Mum? I bet she'd love it."

"OK. Let's see what she thinks." Mum pulled open the freezer door and got out the ice-cube tray.

"While you're there, can I have another lolly?" Oscar asked hopefully.

"No. Here – shall we put them in her water bowl?" Mum squished the tray to get out the ice cubes and stood there with them in her palm. "Ooh, that feels so nice!"

"Let's put one by her nose and one in her bowl." Daisy picked up Betsy's bowl and went to put fresh water in. "Look, she's rolled over again. I think she's feeling a bit better. Here, Betsy, it's lovely and cold now." She put down the bowl next to the little dog, who peered at the ice cube bobbing around. "And here's another one." Daisy laid it between Betsy's paws and she twitched in surprise. "It's nice – try it!"

Betsy sniffed at it suspiciously. Then she scrabbled the ice cube closer with her little ginger paws and tucked it under her chin. Daisy could see the fur slowly darkening as the ice cube melted.

"She'll be OK," Mum said. "You were right to dash home with her, though. Poor Betsy. We'd better watch her carefully over the weekend and not let her stay out in the garden too long."

"I thought we could put her in the paddling pool," Daisy suggested. "It's in the shed. I don't mind pumping it up." She looked out into the garden. "I could even get it out now."

Mum laughed. "Betsy could probably swim in it. Let's see what she thinks tomorrow. Right. Dinner. Your dad'll be home in a minute." She turned to get the plates out of the cupboard and Daisy started to find the cutlery. "It's pasta salad and cold sausages. I couldn't face eating anything hot. Can you get the ketchup out for me?"

Daisy grabbed the ketchup – enjoying the gust

of cold air from the fridge – and then laughed as a small paw patted her foot insistently. Betsy was sitting at her feet, looking hard done by, and Chloe was curled up in Betsy's wet towel, her face pink and her hair in sweaty little ringlets. She seemed to be fast asleep.

"She must have sneaked in here when we weren't looking," Daisy said, rolling her eyes.

"Chloe, love, that was for the dog." Mum sighed. "Oh well. Sorry, Bets. We'll get you another towel…"

After dinner, Daisy wandered upstairs. She
felt restless – at a loose end somehow. It was
because it was still so hot, she decided. She
glanced around the room she shared with
Chloe, at her books and her colouring, the
friendship bracelet she'd started knotting to
send to Mara, but none of it called to her. She
slumped down on her bed and heaved a sigh.
Chloe was downstairs arguing with Mum
about not wanting a bath but Daisy knew she
wouldn't have long on her own. She ought to
make the most of the peace.

Daisy blinked at a thumping sound on the stairs — was that Chloe stomping up already? Then she smiled. Betsy! The little dachshund was too short for the tall steps so she had to scramble and heave herself over them one by one. She appeared in the doorway, panting, and Daisy went to scoop her up.

"You shouldn't have," she murmured affectionately. "You're supposed to be taking it easy." She ran Betsy's silky ears through her fingers. "Did you know I was feeling lonely?"

Betsy reached up, put her paws on Daisy's shoulder and licked her chin. Then she bounced on to the duvet, stamping round and round until she had it arranged just the way she liked it. She curled up into a determined little ball with her nose pressed against Daisy's leg and seemed to go straight to sleep. Daisy sighed again and leaned back against the wall. Betsy couldn't have said it any more clearly.

I don't know what's the matter with you but here I am. And now could you shh?

"I don't really know what the matter is either…" Daisy whispered. She twisted her fingers together in her lap and blinked hard. "OK. Maybe I do. School was horrible – again."

Betsy snuffled and grunted in her sleep but it almost sounded like she was answering.

"Jack Wilson was picking on me again. I nearly cried," Daisy admitted. "He said my furry pencil case was babyish and everyone at my old school must have been stupid if they thought it was cool. He was grinning at me – he thought he was so clever. The girls in my class – you know, Kacie and Skye and the others, they were nice and they told him to get lost. But I just feel so lonely. Everyone else has been at school since Reception and they know each other so well. Sometimes I still don't feel like I belong. I miss Mara all the time. Even when we weren't sitting together, we always did things at break. And we sat next to each other at lunch. Now I haven't got anyone special to sit with."

She ran her hand down Betsy's curled back, feeling the tiny bumps of her spine. "I bet you miss her too," she went on. "Your walk this afternoon would've been more fun if Mara was with us, wouldn't it? You loved Mara. I mean, you love her," Daisy added quickly, with a gulp. "It's not fair that we can't visit her. I can understand dogs not being allowed in a hospital, I suppose. Even though I'm sure you're very clean." Betsy snuffled again and Daisy laughed. "But why not friends?"

Mum had explained that she wasn't allowed to visit as Mara's immune system was weakened because of her cancer treatment. If anyone gave her just the tiniest bit of a cold, her body wouldn't be able to cope. It seemed so unfair. Mara must be so lonely, stuck in hospital. Her mum was there most of the time and she was allowed visits from her little sister, Lucy. But it was family only. No friends from school.

"It would make her feel better if she could see people, I know it would," Daisy muttered. "Isn't being happy supposed to help you get well faster?" She sniffed, and Betsy looked up, yawned and then wriggled round. She rested her chin on Daisy's leg.

"Too hot," Daisy whispered, but she didn't want Betsy to move.

The awful thing was, even if Daisy did get to visit Mara in hospital, she wasn't sure how much she'd be able to cheer up her best friend. She'd only ever been to a hospital once, to visit her grandma after she'd had a hip operation. That had been OK. They'd taken Gran a book and some strawberries because they were her favourite. Daisy and Oscar and Chloe had sat on her bed (very, very carefully). It hadn't been scary, even though Gran was attached to tubes and wires and things. Gran had been just like herself and they'd known she was coming home soon.

Nobody knew when Mara was coming home. Daisy had bothered Mum about it, on and on. *When will she be better? Will Mara be back at school this week? What about half-term, she has to be better by then – it's weeks away!*

In the end Mum had sat down with her – here, on Daisy's bed – and told her that Mara might not get better. They didn't know. They hoped. But her treatment was going to take a long time. All they could do was be there for Mara when she needed them. Mara had gone into hospital during the Easter holidays and now it was nearly the end of the summer term. It seemed long enough to Daisy already.

After that talk with Mum, things had changed. Before, Daisy had chatted to Mara on the phone every couple of days, and sent her pictures and emails – but it felt different talking to her now. Knowing how sick Mara was seemed to have made everything different. Daisy felt scared about talking to her – what if she said the wrong thing? Or Mara said something that made them both sad? She felt like she didn't know what to say any more. And she was sure Mara could tell.

Daisy had stopped calling so often. She still sent photos – that was easier. She sent loads of pictures of Betsy, because Mara adored her. And whenever she went out for walks she tried to take pictures of the New Forest ponies too. Mara was horse-mad. She went riding every weekend – or she used to – and she loved watching the ponies wandering wild through the forest and the villages.

Daisy liked them too – they were beautiful, but she was a bit scared of them sometimes. She supposed it was because she hadn't grown up here, seeing them every day. They were so big and she wasn't sure about them walking about on their own… She sometimes worried that a pony was going to get spooked by her or Betsy and maybe kick out. But Mara had promised her the ponies wouldn't kick unless she crept up and frightened them, and Daisy certainly wasn't going to do that.

Sending pictures wasn't the same as a phone call, though – Daisy knew that. So as well as missing Mara and not enjoying school without her best friend, she felt guilty too. Too guilty to tell anyone about it, even Mum.

She looked down at Betsy, who'd gone back
to sleep again, and leaned carefully sideways so
as not to disturb her. She could just about reach
her desk and the friendship bracelet. Gran
and Grandpa had given her a kit for her
birthday. It had all the threads, and some
charms and beads to weave into the
bracelets too.

She had seen the
tiny silver pony charm
and thought of Mara
at once. It would be
a perfect present to
send to her in hospital.
Making something nice
for Mara might help her
feel less guilty about not
calling too.

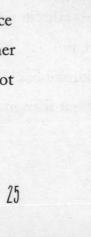

She laid the instructions on her lap and frowned, trying to remember which colour she was supposed to use next. She was making it purple and silver – Mara's favourite colours. That was the problem with starting and stopping – she kept forgetting where she'd got to. She knotted a few more strands and then looked round, hearing Mum and Chloe coming up the stairs.

"Oh, so that's where Betsy is, I should've known," Mum said. "That's pretty, Daisy."

"It's for Mara." Daisy held it up and Mum stroked the fine silk threads.

"It's lovely." She paused, watching Chloe searching grumpily for her pyjamas. "Have you called her today?"

Daisy shook her head. "I'll do it tomorrow."

Mum was silent for a moment and then

she just nodded, as though she wanted to say something, but couldn't work out how. "OK. Well, give her my love." She turned to shoo Chloe towards the bathroom.

"Yeah." Daisy stared down at the bracelet, fighting not to cry.

3

Daisy made herself call Mara the next day. It wasn't that she didn't want to talk to her, of course she did. But she wanted her friend to sound the same as before – so funny and determined – and she knew Mara wouldn't.

"So Miss Fondu said we should leave Kacie there. All the way through the literacy lesson. She didn't wake up until lunch." She paused for a moment, hoping Mara would laugh. Or even just smile – Daisy was sure she could tell when someone was smiling down the phone. But there was only silence on the other end.

"Um, are you still there?" she asked, hesitating.

"Yeah…" A faint, soft murmur.

"Good… Anyway, I was surprised Miss Fondu let her stay asleep – she's usually so strict. But it is nearly the last week of term, I suppose." Then she caught her breath. Mum had warned her not to say anything that might make Mara feel bad about missing school, or remind her how long she'd been away. But the only thing Daisy had to talk about was school. How was she supposed to not mention it? "Sorry," she muttered, but Mara didn't say anything. Daisy wasn't even sure if she was listening.

"Has … has anything happened with you…?" she asked. Mara had a teacher who came round to her in the hospital. She'd said he was nicer than Miss Fondu. She'd been given books from

the hospital school, but she wasn't well enough
to actually go to it. "I guess not…" she muttered.
It had been a bit of a stupid question. But Daisy
couldn't think of anything else to say.

"Oh! Did you know there's a tree not far
from our house that's actually two trees stuck
together?" she said quickly. "My dad showed
me the other day when we were walking Betsy.
It's an oak and … a beech tree, I think? And
they've grown together into one tree. Isn't that
weird? Have you seen it?"

"I think so," Mara mumbled, and Daisy held
back a sigh. Mara didn't seem to be interested
in anything she was saying.

"Um. Have you watched any more films?"

"No… Been really tired."

"Oh… So … shall I go then? I can call you
again tomorrow? Or in a couple of days?"

She was almost sure she could feel Mara's relief – Mara wanted her gone. She knew it was only because Mara was so tired, but it still felt horrible. Daisy didn't know what to say. "OK. Um. Bye." She ended the call and sat staring at the phone, warm in her hand. What had just happened? She'd had calls with Mara before where it was hard to find stuff to talk about, but never anything like that.

"Oh, you've finished!" Chloe erupted into the room and danced up and down in front of her. "Come and play UNO! Mum said I had to wait until you weren't on the phone, but you aren't now so you have to play with me."

"Leave me alone, Chloe!" Daisy snapped. She couldn't cope with her little sister bouncing around right now.

"You have to! Mum said!"

"No!" Daisy yelled. She knew she was going to get into trouble, but she was past caring. "Go away! Stop being such a pain!" She watched Chloe's face crumple – she could almost see the wail building up inside her.

"Mu-u-um!" Chloe disappeared, stumbling down the stairs in noisy tears, and Daisy slumped on her bed. Why was it her fault? Why should she always have to play with Chloe? Couldn't Oscar, or Dad or Mum?

She counted in her head, wondering how long it would take for Mum to appear in her room. About fifty seconds as it turned out.

"What was that all about?" Mum asked. Her voice was mild but Daisy could tell she was annoyed.

"She said I had to play with her…" Daisy muttered. "I just didn't want to. Why do I always have to?"

"Because she's your sister!"

"So?"

"Daisy!" Mum glared at her, and then sighed and sat down on the bed. "What happened? You were talking to Mara, weren't you? Has she – has she had bad news?"

Daisy stared at Mum, her eyes widening. "No… What do you mean? What sort of bad news? Has Mara's mum said something to you?"

Mum put her arm round Daisy and squeezed her. "No, it's OK. I haven't heard anything. I just wondered if that's why you were upset."

"I'm not upset," Daisy growled, but it wasn't worth pretending. Mum didn't say anything, and after a while Daisy whispered, "I didn't know what to say to her. It doesn't feel the same, talking to her."

Mum hugged her tighter. "It's bound to be difficult, love. And I'm sure Mara appreciates you calling, even if it doesn't sound like it. Perhaps she's had a bad night. She really needs you, you know."

But what about me? Daisy wanted to shout. *What about what I need? I don't have my best friend any more and I hate it!*

She couldn't say it out loud though. Not without Mum thinking she was a selfish monster. Because she was a selfish monster, thinking like that when Mara was so ill.

"Look, I'll take care of Chloe," Mum whispered into Daisy's hair. "Keep her occupied. Maybe she can play outside with your dad, or I'll fill up the paddling pool. Do you want to stay up here? Or go out? It's still hot but not nearly as bad as yesterday. You could take Betsy for a walk."

"Yeah." Daisy nodded, rubbing her cheek against Mum's arm. "Good idea." Just her and Betsy, walking through the forest. She could try not to imagine Mara dashing along in front.

Mum gave her one last squeeze and stood up, and Daisy followed her wearily. She ached but she didn't know why. She followed Mum downstairs and ignored Chloe scowling at her.

Betsy bustled out from the kitchen looking

hopeful when she heard Daisy take her lead off its hook.

"Don't go far," Dad said, following her to the door. "Take some water, for both of you."

Daisy nodded and held up her backpack. "I've got water in here."

"And your phone? Have you got battery?"

"Yes, Dad."

"I want to go with Daisy!" Chloe moaned.

"You're going to help me cut the grass!" Dad said, putting on a hurt face. "I need you!"

Chloe eyed him suspiciously but Daisy knew she loved throwing the cut grass around. She gave in after a few seconds and Daisy let herself out of the front door, with Betsy already tugging excitedly at her lead.

"Slow down," she told the dachshund as Betsy raced along the pavement. "You're not getting in a state like you did yesterday. This is a slow walk. More of a sit."

The problem was that even if Daisy walked slowly, Betsy didn't. Daisy didn't ever let her off the lead, because Betsy's recall was useless. As far as she was concerned, if she spotted something interesting, like another dog or some litter to eat, why would she want to come back? Dad had taken her to dog-training but they'd never exactly been the stars of the class. So they'd got Betsy a long lead instead and she made the most of it. She would do her funny bouncing run backwards and forwards at the length of the lead, going about three times the distance Daisy walked. It was hard to stop her wearing herself out.

"You're supposed to be taking it easy," Daisy sighed as Betsy wandered off to sniff at some foxgloves. "If you get overheated again you'll be sorry!" Then she stopped, pulling at Betsy's lead. "Hey, Betsy, wait… Look…"

They were walking along the wide path leading out through the trees to the heathland, not far from the house. Daisy still thought it was strange, going from her house on a paved street in the village to the wild heath in only minutes. The heather was coming out now and the patch of heath beyond the trees was covered in clumps of pinky-purple flowers, stretching away for what looked like miles. Tiny footpaths wove in and out of the heather, and Betsy loved to shoot along them in great bouncing leaps.

But it was a whitish patch under the trees close by that had caught Daisy's eye. It had taken a moment or two to work out what it was, for her eyes to understand what she was seeing – a white pony, nibbling at the lower branches of a holly tree. Now she was really looking, Daisy saw there were more of them. A chestnut pony, over on the other side of the holly – and another smaller chestnut cropping a patch of grass. The smaller one didn't look like a normal chestnut though, with its long pale mane. Mara would know what that was called.

Usually Daisy would have admired the ponies
– from a safe distance – and then walked on,
but this time she stayed. They'd made her
think of Mara. Now she'd have something to
tell her about in their next phone call. She
could ask Mara what a chestnut pony with a
pretty blond mane was called.

"Shh," she murmured to Betsy. "Let's sit here
for a bit, OK?" She crouched down by the
foxgloves, stroking Betsy's head to calm her.
"Good dog." Slowly, Daisy sat cross-legged on
the short, worn turf, peering carefully through
the tall pink flowers at the ponies.

Betsy sat and panted beside her. She'd
noticed the ponies too, Daisy could see her
watching them, but the dachshund didn't seem
to be very bothered. She'd seen ponies before
and she never tried to chase them, or say hello,

like she did with other dogs. It was as if she thought they were too big to be interesting.

It was very soothing, listening to Betsy huffing away and watching the ponies. She could hear someone calling too, a little way off, and the faint buzz of cars on the road that ran past her house. Every so often there was a little thud as one of the ponies moved a step, or a creaking noise as they pulled at a stubborn bit of holly. At last the two chestnut ponies shook themselves and moved on, stopping here and there to nibble a good patch of grass, and gradually disappearing out on to the heath among the heather.

The white pony... Except it was called a grey, Daisy remembered now. She'd argued with Mara about that because they weren't grey, they were white. This one was so pale that she

looked almost silvery – she seemed to glow.
The white pony stayed by the holly, gradually
moving round to eat the young shoots. Dad had
explained to her when they first moved here that
New Forest ponies ate all sorts of things that
normal ponies might not – holly and prickly
gorse. They had specially adapted mouths, with
thicker lips so they could manage the spiky
plants. The trees here had trunks that were bare
all the way up to where the ponies could reach.

Beside her, Betsy yawned loudly and the white
pony slowly turned to look at them. Daisy was
sure she'd already known that they were there
but the ponies were used to people being around
in the forest. This one had probably been
photographed hundreds of times – she was so
pretty, with her dark eyes and the messy fringe
hanging over her nose. Daisy smiled to herself.

Fringe wasn't right. Mara would be jumping up and down telling her it was a forelock. Or something like that. But it looked like a fringe, a fair, tangled one. Actually, just like Mara's. She was trying to grow it out and she was always pushing it out of her eyes.

Daisy swallowed. She wasn't now. Mara had told Daisy about a month ago that her hair was falling out because of the treatment she was having. All that time trying to get rid of her fringe wasted. She'd been so cross about it.

The pony had dark grey ears and a few darker spots dappling her chest. Daisy didn't think she'd seen any others like that. Slowly, carefully, she reached into her shorts pocket for her phone to take a photo. She didn't have to say anything to Mara about the fringe – she could just tell her she'd seen this pretty pony.

The pony didn't seem bothered by the click of the camera. She wandered away from the holly sapling and started to graze, slowly nibbling at the grass. But every so often, she lifted her head to look back at them.

The pony was just keeping an eye on Betsy, Daisy told herself. She wanted to make sure that Betsy wasn't going to dash at her and start yapping. Still, it did feel like the pony was checking on Daisy too. As if she knew something wasn't quite right, that Daisy was unhappy. Her dark eyes were so gentle when she looked over her shoulder like that. She seemed to be making sure Daisy was OK.

Daisy found herself smiling. It was silly – but she was going to carry on thinking it anyway.

4

"You're going out again?" Dad asked the next
afternoon, looking surprised. "You took Betsy
for a long walk this morning!"

"She always likes more walks," Daisy pointed
out. Dad usually took Betsy for a quick walk
before he went to work, and Daisy tried to fit
in one after school, but at weekends and in
the holidays, Betsy got lots of extras. "I want
to find some ponies too. I need to send some
photos to Mara."

She twisted her fingers behind her back – it
was true but it wasn't quite the whole truth.

She wanted to see if she could find that white pony again. There was something about her — something that had made Daisy feel so much better the day before. She hadn't sent the photo to Mara yet, though. She'd been about to send the email but then she'd deleted it. That strange connection with the white pony felt like her secret.

"OK…" Dad looked thoughtful. "Lucky Betsy. Don't let her get too close to any ponies, will you? I'm not sure I trust her to be sensible. You know she thinks she's loads bigger than she is."

"I'm not going near them either," Daisy promised. "I just want to take pictures."

And watch. And hope for that same feeling I got yesterday.

How far did the ponies walk in a day? Daisy wasn't sure. Although the New Forest ponies

did have owners, they were almost wild. They
didn't have fields or a stable to go back to
at night – they could wander wherever they
wanted to go. There were some favourite
places, where you could almost always see
them, like the middle of Burley village where
they always looked like they wanted the
visitors' picnics. But you couldn't really count
on them being around, just like any other wild
creature. The white pony had been close to the
house yesterday but that didn't mean she would
be again.

"Maybe she likes it in this bit of the forest,"
she suggested hopefully to Betsy as they
headed along the path. "They looked happy,
didn't they?" She sighed. "I wish I could put
down treats for her. I mean, she'd probably
like an apple, or a carrot but Mum and

Dad said we mustn't ever feed them because they're wild."

No one was supposed to feed the ponies, in case people decided to start feeding them things that were bad for them, like crisps or chocolate. And it would make them want to come closer to busy places, where they were more likely to get hit by a car. Daisy knew that made sense but it did seem sad. She loved the thought of that white pony lipping an apple out of her hand.

She giggled to herself. She'd never wanted one of them to come that close to her before. Ponies were big – and so were their teeth… On second thoughts, she still wasn't sure she really did want the white pony that close.

Betsy wasn't listening to Daisy chattering on about ponies. She was enjoying her second

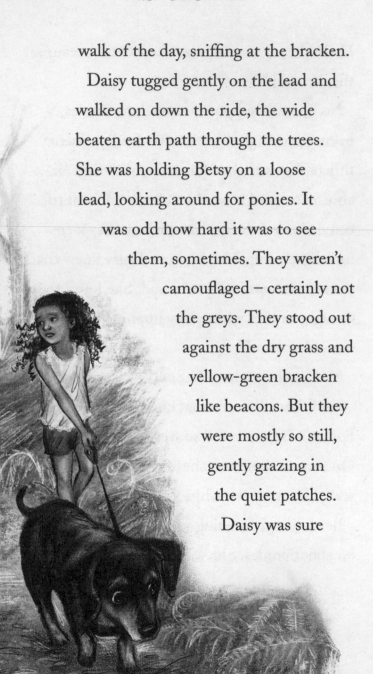

walk of the day, sniffing at the bracken.
Daisy tugged gently on the lead and
walked on down the ride, the wide
beaten earth path through the trees.
She was holding Betsy on a loose
lead, looking around for ponies. It
was odd how hard it was to see
them, sometimes. They weren't
camouflaged – certainly not
the greys. They stood out
against the dry grass and
yellow-green bracken
like beacons. But they
were mostly so still,
gently grazing in
the quiet patches.
Daisy was sure

she'd walked past hundreds of ponies and never known they were there.

"Where are you?" she said sadly. The white pony could be miles and miles away by now.

A faint rustling among the trees made Daisy spin round, hoping to see the pony's white face peering out from behind a tree trunk – but instead a small herd of fallow deer stared back at her. They looked a bit surprised, their heads held up as if they were about to dash away any second.

"Sorry," Daisy whispered, taking a tighter grip on Betsy's lead. She'd never seen deer so close and neither had Betsy. The deer were usually shyer than the ponies and their dappled-brown coats meant they melted into the landscape. She was lucky to see them – usually she'd have been really excited.

Betsy was wagging her tail wildly and her
ears had lifted – they'd have been pricked up
if they weren't so long and floppy.

"You can't chase them," Daisy told her
sternly, and the deer caught the sound of her
voice and twitched. As one, they turned and
stepped hurriedly away through the trees.

"Oh... I didn't mean to scare them off!"
Daisy sighed. "And we still haven't seen a
single pony. I didn't see any this morning,

either." She checked the time on her phone.
"We should head back, Betsy-dog. Dad'll be
worrying about us."

"Last week at school," Mum said
encouragingly the next morning. "It's going
to be hot again. I put your water bottles in the
freezer last night."

Daisy nodded. The mum of one of Oscar's
friends had suggested that when they were
walking home on Friday. Maybe she could put
the icy bottle on her table at school and hug it
while she was trying to listen to Miss Fondu.

"And there's loads of fruit in your lunches,"
Mum added, looking at Oscar worriedly.
He didn't sleep well in the heat and he looked
like he was about to faceplant into his cereal.

"Finish it up, Oscar. We need to get going."

Even opening the front door felt like being hit with a wall of heat and they straggled limply out on to the pavement. It wasn't a long walk to school, luckily, just ten minutes to the other end of the village, past the shops.

Daisy was eyeing the newsagent's window, wondering whether they could convince Mum they needed ice cream for a second breakfast, when Chloe squeaked and pointed ahead.

Mum started to laugh. "Oh, look. They want

a cut and blow dry."

On the other side of the road, standing on the pavement and apparently very interested in the posters in the hairdresser's window, were three ponies. A chestnut, a young chestnut with a pale mane, and a white pony with a messy fringe and dark grey ears. The three of them turned round curiously to look at Chloe squealing and jumping up and down.

It was her pony!

"I saw them when I took Betsy out on Saturday," she told Mum, a bubble of happiness rising inside her. "The same three. Perhaps they're going to stay around."

"They're very sweet," Mum said. "Especially that little chestnut one with the blond mane."

"He's mine," Chloe said, pointing. "My pony. Oscar can have the big brown one and the white one's for Daisy."

Daisy stared at her sister, blinking silently. Chloe said silly stuff all the time, nonsense words and little songs she'd made up but she sounded so serious now that it felt real. Of course the white pony wasn't really Daisy's and Chloe would have forgotten about them by the time she got to nursery.

But the happy bubble inside Daisy was growing, faster and faster, as if it was filling up a hole.

After that, it was as if the pony knew that Daisy was looking for her. Some days she was there when Daisy went out exploring the woods over the next few weeks, and some days she wasn't, but Daisy saw her often enough that she began to feel like a friend. Too much of a friend just to be called 'the white pony'. Daisy was sure that the pony recognized her now. She would turn and watch her, and sometimes she wandered a few steps towards Daisy and Betsy, giving them a friendly, interested sort of look. Daisy wanted so much to stroke her but she never did.

"I could call you Mara," Daisy said, leaning against the trunk of a tree and watching the white pony graze. "Your fringe still reminds me

of her, you know. You make me think of her.
You make me think of Mara, how she used to
be," she added in a whisper.

The white pony went on placidly munching
grass. The weather had broken at the start
of the summer holidays, which Daisy's mum
said was typical. Today was a showery sort of
day, and Betsy had got three steps out of the
front door and gone on a sit-down strike. She
didn't like rain – it splashed up on her tummy,
and she got soaked and cold so quickly. She'd
scuttled back inside and Daisy had gone out
pony-watching on her own, in a waterproof
and wellies. The ponies looked pretty wet too,
but they didn't seem to mind, and at least the
grass was a bit greener and nicer now.

"I called her again yesterday," she told the
pony. "But Mara's mum answered her phone.

She said Mara wasn't feeling great and she
was asleep. And it was the same last time. I
haven't talked to her properly for a whole week
and that time she had to go after a couple
of minutes because there was a doctor who
needed to see her." She kicked at the grass with
her boot. "I still haven't sent her any photos of
you. I did tell her we saw three ponies by the
hairdresser's, though, like they were going for
a haircut, and she thought that was funny. She
said some ponies get their manes plaited for
shows. And you have to French plait the fringe
bit." She squinted at the white pony's forelock.
"I don't see how, to be honest, but Mara said
it's the best way to make a pony neat and tidy.
I think you'd look weird."

The pony turned to look at her, chewing
thoughtfully, and Daisy shook her head.

"No, it would be strange if you were called Mara too. I'd mix you up. I suppose you have a name already. Whoever it is you belong to must have given you a name, even if they don't see you all that often." Daisy hesitated, biting her bottom lip. "It doesn't matter. I can have my own name for you. Maybe Lily? Bella?"

Daisy gazed at the pony, hoping she might make some sort of sign, but she just wandered off to the other side of the tree to nibble at a clump of longer grass. "The thing is, I suppose I've already sort of been calling you Mara in my head and now the other names don't feel right. Something else beginning with 'm' perhaps. Milly?"

The pony peered back round the tree, looking a bit ditzy, and Daisy laughed. "Muppet! No, that's mean. M... M..."

The pony's grey ears pricked forward and Daisy nodded. "You like that? I could call you that. Em. Like short for Emily."

The pony stepped delicately round the tree, closer to Daisy, and Daisy held her breath. Her greyish-white nose looked so soft, spiked with short little whiskers, and Daisy ached to stroke her. She'd never come so near, not in all the times Daisy had watched her. It felt like a sign.

"Hi, Em," she whispered.

That night, Daisy just couldn't seem to get to sleep. She glanced across the room at her little sister, who was asleep on her back and making funny little whistling noises, then dangled over the side of her bed, feeling around for her torch. She was sure it was under there somewhere.

It was! She turned it on, cautiously watching Chloe – but she didn't stir.

Daisy pulled her drawing pad over from her desk, and some coloured pencils, and started to draw. She wasn't very good at drawing ponies – the legs were really hard to do – but what she wanted to draw was Em's face when she'd been looking round that tree. She'd come so close, she'd almost looked like she wanted to bump noses. She'd gazed at Daisy for a moment more, and then turned and wandered away into the wood. Daisy was sure she could remember how her eyes had looked, the way she'd peered through that messy fall of white hair. She'd seemed so curious, so friendly.

Daisy looked down at her drawing and sighed. It wasn't quite right. Em didn't look as intelligent as she did for real, or as special. But it was close.

It had been true, what Daisy had said to
Em earlier on. The pony did make her think
of Mara, with her funny fringe and dark eyes.
Talking to Em almost felt more like talking
to Mara than talking to the real Mara did –
at the moment.

That wasn't fair.

Slowly, Daisy wrote across
the bottom of the page.

*This is a pony I keep seeing
in the forest close to our house. She makes me
think of you and how you love ponies!
See you soon I hope.
Daisy xxx*

5

"Hey…" Daisy answered her phone a little doubtfully, unsure what to expect. Usually it was her ringing Mara, not the other way around. Mara had still been so quiet and sleepy the last time they'd spoken, and then over the last few days her mum had kept answering her phone for her.

"I love her! She's so pretty! Where did you see her?"

"Oh! You got my picture? I only put it through your door yesterday – I wasn't sure when you'd see it."

"Mum brought it in to show me earlier.
I didn't know you could draw horses like
that, Daisy!"

Daisy felt her ears turn pink and she grinned
into the phone. It was so good to hear Mara
sounding awake and bouncy again. "Thanks.
I can't do the legs, though," she admitted. "I
keep seeing that pony along the paths near
our house. She's usually with a chestnut, and
another chestnut who's got a cream-coloured
mane and tail – the same ones
I told you about that were
by the hairdresser's.
I called her Em,
like 'm' for Mara,
because she
reminded me
of you—"

Suddenly remembering that she didn't want
to remind Mara about losing her hair, she added
quickly, "You know, loving ponies so much."

"I really miss riding." Mara sighed. "Have
you got any photos of her? Will you send them
to me, Daisy, pleeeaaase? I've got a board I can
stick pictures up on. Mum can print them out
for me."

"Sure." Daisy was silent for a moment, not
sure whether she ought to say anything. But
she had to. "It's so nice talking to you," she
mumbled. "I miss you."

"I miss you." Mara sniffed. "The doctors
told me I should be able to have visitors soon.
Maybe in a couple of days. Will you come?"

"Definitely!"

"OK. Cool. I have to go now but please send
me the photos?"

"I will, I promise. And I'll come and visit you. Bye!" Daisy sat holding her phone, staring at it and smiling. That had felt like talking to Mara, the old Mara. And it was all because of Em. She opened up the photos on her phone, flicking through her pictures of the white pony. Em was keeping her and Mara together.

"Can you see her?" Daisy murmured to Betsy, looking out for a flash of white coat as they wandered along the path. "Oh, I think I can see the chestnut ones." Mara had emailed her straight back when she'd sent the photos of the ponies, saying the chestnut with the pale mane was called a flaxen chestnut. And that Em was beautiful. Daisy was hoping to get a good close-up of Em to send her.

The chestnut pony was out on the heath, and Daisy was pretty sure she could see Em and the flaxen chestnut a little bit beyond, knee-deep in pink heather. She was about to make her way over to them, when she caught a flash of yellow. Someone else was already there – right up close to the ponies.

No one was supposed to get that close to them! All the signs said, *Look but don't touch.* Daisy hesitated at the edge of the trees, wondering what to do. Should she go and tell them? But they might not listen to a ten-year-old…

"Shh, it's OK," she murmured to Betsy, who was tugging on the lead, clearly not sure why they'd stopped. "Just wait a minute." Betsy sighed loudly and sat down on the grass, idly scratching at one of her ears. "Hey… Is that…?" Daisy stepped back, almost tripping on Betsy's

lead. "Sorry, sorry… Are you OK?"
She crouched down to fuss over the
indignant little dog, but she was still
peering through the trees at the boy in the
yellow T-shirt.

A boy that she knew.

"What's he doing here? Why's he with
Em?" Daisy said angrily. "He shouldn't be
messing around with her like that!"

The boy in the yellow T-shirt was Jack Wilson from her class. Daisy couldn't stand him. He still picked on her almost every day. He made faces whenever she had to talk in class and he rubbished everything she said. Even when she was just answering the register, he managed to make her sound like an idiot. Daisy had no idea why. He just seemed to like making fun of her. It was yet another reason she missed Mara being around. Mara had always stuck up for her – although she did tell Daisy off afterwards.

"You let him get to you!" she said. "If you didn't show him you minded, he wouldn't bother doing it."

It was all very well saying that but how was Daisy supposed to pretend that she didn't care, when she did? When the whole class was

sniggering at her and even Miss Fondu looked
as though she was trying not to laugh?

Jack was funny, everybody thought so.
Without Mara there, Daisy just stared at
the tabletop and tried to imagine she was
somewhere else.

And now Jack Wilson – mean, cruel,
horrible Jack Wilson – was standing right
next to Em. Petting her nose! Touching her,
when everyone said you were never, ever
supposed to touch the ponies.

On one of the last days that Mara had been
in school – when she'd been off sick a day here
and a day there, and her mum thought she
had some sort of nasty virus that wouldn't go
away – she'd had a massive row with Jack about
Daisy. They'd been skipping in the playground
with a long rope that Skye had brought in.

Almost all the girls in the class were playing,
running in and out, doing a figure of eight
and then chanting *Bluebells, cockleshells, eevy,
ivy, over*. They hadn't skipped for a while and
everyone kept tripping. Lots of the girls did
– so when Daisy got tangled in the rope, Jack
didn't need to start laughing and pointing and
whispering to his friends.

"Shut up and leave her alone!" Mara had
snarled, hauling Daisy out of the way of the
others. "Are you OK? I said shut up!" she
added, rounding on Jack again. "Go and jump
off a cliff!"

"Awww. Can't Daisy talk for herself? Why
does she always need you to stick up for
her?" Jack was smirking, looking over his
shoulder at his mates, checking that his
audience was there.

Mara had nudged Daisy in the ribs – a go on, say something sign. But all Daisy could manage was, "Leave me alone," in a weak sort of mumble.

"Leave me aloooooone!" Jack parroted. "Awww, she wants us to leave her alone."

"Get lost!" Mara had yelled. She was seething and the worst thing was, Daisy had been pretty sure that Mara was almost as cross with her as she was with Jack. Daisy had slunk away and sat on one of the benches pretending she'd hurt her knee when she tripped and didn't want to skip any more. She did. She just didn't want to do it with Jack and his gang watching.

What she should have done was said something like, *Go on, you do it then, let's see how good you are*. Except Jack would probably be brilliant at skipping. He was always playing football, and Mara had told her he went to the same riding school that she did, and he won prizes and things. So she'd just have looked even more useless.

The unfairness of it surged up inside her again now and she marched out on to the heath, with a surprised Betsy stumbling after her.

"Hey! You leave her alone! You aren't supposed to touch the ponies!"

She wasn't quite as loud as she'd meant to be but Jack turned round. "What?" he called back, and then, "Oh, it's you."

There was something about the way he said the word *you* that made Daisy furious. He sounded exactly like he did when he spoke to her at school, as though she was nothing.

"Get away from her!" she screamed, startling Betsy. The little dog cowered down against the

grass with a tiny whimper. She wasn't used
to hearing Daisy shout like that, not ever.
The ponies were shocked too. Em whinnied
and laid back her ears, and Daisy felt a hot
rush of shame running over her. She'd scared
the ponies and her own Betsy. But it wasn't
her fault. It was Jack's – he'd started it.

"Get away!" she yelled again, louder and higher, and this time the ponies startled and trotted away, leaving Jack standing by himself in the heather.

"What did you do that for?" he said, stomping towards her. "You scared them! You don't scream like that around ponies! You could've got yourself kicked! Or me!"

"Like you know so much about ponies," Daisy muttered. A tiny little bit of her deep inside was thinking, *I'm arguing back! I'm shouting at him! What would Mara say?* She'd just never been angry enough before. "You're not supposed to touch them – there's a sign literally over there that says so!" She waved at it and Jack stared at her.

"That's for the tourists," he said, shaking his head as if she was stupid. "It doesn't mean me!"

"Because you're so special?" Daisy was so cross now that she was practically shaking. Betsy was whining, and looking between her and Jack with the whites of her eyes showing.

"Sorry, sorry, it's OK," Daisy whispered, picking her up. "It's OK." She forced herself to breathe in slowly, the way Miss Fondu had told her to do once, when she was upset at school. It had helped her stop crying and she guessed it might help make her less angry too.

"I never said I was special," Jack said, rolling his eyes. "But I'm definitely allowed to touch her since SHE BELONGS TO MY DAD!"

Daisy felt the bottom drop out of her stomach. All of her went cold, all at once.

Jack folded his arms and smirked – the same way he did when he was teasing her at school. For a moment Daisy thought she was going to cry and run away like she usually did but she could hear Mara in her head, going, *Why don't you say something back? Don't just cry!*

"Why didn't you say so then?" she snapped, and she had the satisfaction of seeing him look surprised.

"I just did! What am I supposed to do, carry around a sign that says, *this is my pony*? I was checking on her!"

"Why?" Daisy demanded.

"Because we have to. We have to make sure they're OK. If they get sick or they're hurt we have to take them in off the forest. To the paddock by our house. Me or Dad, we check on them every couple of days. Don't you know anything?"

Daisy wanted to answer him back but she couldn't. She *didn't* know anything. "I hate you," she hissed. It was all she could think of to say and it was true.

"I'm so scared." Jack leaned down and picked up a green plastic bucket that had been by his feet – Daisy hadn't even noticed it. "Mind if I go and feed the foal now? Is that allowed?" He shook his head disgustedly and marched off after the ponies, leaving Daisy standing shaking in the heather.

It took a good five minutes of slow breathing, and letting Betsy lick her cheek and scrabble at her with tiny paws, before Daisy could turn and walk back to the ride.

I haven't even got any more photos for Mara, Daisy thought miserably as she headed back home. And then all at once her knees gave way and she slumped down on the grass. She hadn't cried at all while she was fighting with Jack but she couldn't hold back her tears any longer. Em was her special link to Mara. She was named for Mara! Except she wasn't, because she must have some other awful wrong name that Jack's family had given her. She wasn't Em at all.

"Sorry," she whispered to Betsy, who was frantically squirming in her lap, jumping up and whining and licking away her tears. "It wasn't much of a walk, was it? We'll get up in a minute, OK?" She gave a huge sniff. "I'm not telling Mara that Em belongs to Jack Wilson. I'm not going to spoil it for her..."

Em wasn't really the thing that had made Mara so much better – well enough that she could have visitors soon. Daisy did know that. But it felt as if the white pony had drawn her and Mara together, after they'd grown apart. Daisy couldn't bear to lose her old, funny, happy Mara when she'd only just got her back again. Jack Wilson wasn't going to ruin that. She couldn't let him.

"Em doesn't belong to Jack's family," Daisy muttered, clutching Betsy so tight she squirmed. "She just doesn't. I suppose there's a piece of paper that says she does but I don't care. She's ours, mine and Mara's."

It was all very well saying it, and Daisy kept repeating the words over and over as they half ran back through the trees, "She's ours. She is. She's ours." But ever since she'd first seen Em, she'd had a memory-picture of her, the white pony with the messy fringe. It had been deep down inside her and she could see Em whenever she wanted.

In her imagination, Daisy was stroking Em's whiskery grey nose and Em had her eyes half closed as if she was so happy. Mara was there too, patting Em's neck. She was a bit hard to see but that was only because the pony was in between them. She was there – Daisy knew it.

The picture didn't feel the same any more. Em was still there but she wasn't looking at Daisy. It was Jack who was patting her nose and Mara had disappeared.

Daisy was determined that Jack wasn't going to spoil things. She'd only fallen in love with the ponies this summer but now they felt like the most important part of the forest for her. She noticed them all, not just Em and her little herd. She was starting to see the differences in them, the way they stood, what they liked to eat. She could tell the different ways their tails were trimmed, to show which part of the forest their owners lived in. When she was out in the car with Mum or Dad, she sometimes spotted ponies that she was sure she'd seen when she was walking Betsy and it made her feel like she belonged. No one was going to take that away.

But she couldn't help looking out for Jack now, whenever she took Betsy for a walk. She didn't want another argument – especially since last time he'd been right. Still, he couldn't stop her watching the ponies, Daisy told herself, even if Em did belong to his family. The forest was free for everyone to walk in. She avoided going out straight after lunch, which was when she'd run into Jack last time. If he always went to see the ponies around then, she'd make sure she missed him.

It was almost a week after their fight, about halfway through the summer holidays, when she saw Jack again. She'd taken Betsy out for an early morning walk and had stopped to watch Em eating gorse from the bushes that bordered the heathland. Even though she knew about the ponies' special mouths, it still made Daisy shudder when she saw them eating the prickly gorse.

She and Oscar had made a cave inside a gorse bush once – it had big holes in it that you could crawl through like tunnels and they'd called it their secret den. They'd hidden from Mum, though looking back Daisy realized she'd known exactly where they were or she'd have been more panicked. Finally they'd come out of their secret hiding place covered in scratches and Oscar had made a hole in his T-shirt. What would gorse do to the inside of someone's mouth? But the ponies didn't seem to have any problems.

"Here, look," she murmured to Betsy. "Let's sit up here." She wasn't very good at climbing

trees but every so often she came across one
that was too good not to climb. The first
branch was so low she could practically step on
to it, with Betsy in her arms, and there was a
smooth piece of bark just right to lean against.
Betsy wriggled but once they were sitting
down she settled for sniffing all round the
branch and then decided that she quite liked
being high up. The little dog sat in her lap like
a queen as Daisy peered down at Em, who was
ignoring their silly antics.

It was so peaceful up there, quiet enough
to hear the bees humming in the gorse and
Em chewing her prickly mouthfuls. Quiet
enough to hear soft footsteps scuffing over
the grass. Daisy froze, pressing herself in tight
against the bark. If she didn't move, hopefully
he wouldn't spot her. Luckily Betsy was half

asleep and all she did was open one eye to see who was coming.

Jack had a bucket with him again. Daisy supposed that was the feed he'd mentioned – the smaller flaxen chestnut pony was the foal he was feeding up. Before he'd said it, she hadn't realized that the flaxen chestnut was only a baby. Jack stopped to talk to Em first, though, and the pony stepped towards him, nudging him with her nose and letting him gently clap her neck.

She was trying to get in the bucket, and Jack laughed and held it behind his back. "Get out of it, Snowball!" he said, pushing her nose.

Snowball! That was Em's real name? Daisy felt like kicking the tree. She watched, blinking angry hot tears, as Jack gave Em a bit of carrot out of his pocket. The white pony crunched the carrot eagerly but it wasn't just the food she wanted. Daisy could see that.

Em – Snowball – she liked him. She was gazing hopefully at him, and when he scratched under her messy fringe she stood with her head lowered, looking blissful. Jack smiled lovingly as he patted her nose and scratched her itches – and when he'd finished, he leaned his cheek against the grey-white dapples of her neck and closed his eyes, just for a second.

Daisy had to look away, she felt so jealous. She kept stone-still as he started to feed the foal. He fussed over her, talking to her gently and praising her for eating it all up.

"Aren't you clever? Clever girl, Acorn! She's getting big, isn't she, Bracken? You're such a good mum, aren't you?"

The ponies all had names then. Daisy bit her lip. They really did belong to him.

"It suits you," Mara said, grinning at Daisy. "It's your colour."

Daisy made a face but she didn't mind the weird green plastic apron covering her clothes. It was to make things as safe as possible for Mara and Daisy wanted to do everything right. Mara sounded chirpy, almost like she did before this all started, but she looked so pale and thin. Dad always teased Daisy and Oscar and Chloe when they were sick, saying that they looked as if a gust of wind would blow them over. Daisy had never seen anyone who looked as if they really would blow over in a strong wind but Mara seemed so fragile. Daisy could see the veins under her skin.

Mara patted the bed next to her. "Sit next to me. Have you got your phone? Can I see the pony photos again?"

Daisy almost didn't want to. What if she hurt her? Mara looked like she might break if Daisy sat down too hard. Her mum and Mara's had gone to the café to get drinks for everyone – if something went wrong, Daisy was the only one there.

"Don't look at me like that!" Mara said, and Daisy froze.

"Like what…" she muttered, trying not to sound guilty.

"Like you're scared to be near me. It's not catching!"

"It wasn't that!" Daisy shook her head earnestly. "It's just…"

"What?" Mara snapped. "Is it because of my hair?"

"No! It's – it's just that you look sick," Daisy tried to explain. "I mean – I knew you were…"

"Yeah, I've been in hospital for months," Mara pointed out icily.

"But I hadn't seen you! Don't be angry, Mara. I'm worried about you, that's all!" Daisy could feel her voice choking up inside her. This wasn't how she wanted things to go.

She'd been so excited to see Mara at last and now she was ruining it. "And it isn't because of your hair – of course it isn't! I like the scarf thing anyway."

"Mum got me lots of them," Mara said, a bit sulkily. She pulled at the bandana covering her head – she was making sure it was on properly, Daisy guessed. Then suddenly Daisy realized she was twirling the curly end of her own dark braid around her finger and stopped as if it had bitten her.

She sat down on the end of Mara's bed cautiously but trying not to look as though she was being careful. "Um. Ponies?" she said hopefully, holding up her phone.

Mara nodded. "You'll have to come closer," she said sternly as if it was a test, and Daisy nodded. Mara was being snappy and bossy and

argumentative like she always had been.
It made her seem a lot less poorly.

Daisy edged further up the bed and leaned
against the stack of pillows next to Mara,
opening up her phone. "Here, look. I took this
one along the ride that runs past the back of
our house, you know? Oh, that's just Betsy
being cute…"

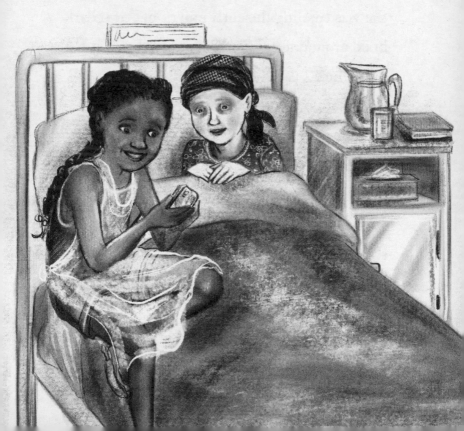

"Your photos are all of Betsy or ponies," Mara said a few minutes later, laughing.

"Yeah, well, yours would be the same except no dog," Daisy pointed out. She didn't realize what she'd said until she glanced at Mara's stricken face. "Sorry…" she whispered.

Mara shrugged. "I took a few of me and the nurses. But I didn't want photos of this place." She waved at the hospital room. "Mum takes loads of pictures anyway."

"Because I think we'll want to remember it one day, when you're home," Mara's mum said, coming back in with a tray.

After that there wasn't as much chance to talk. Daisy could see Mara's mum watching them as if she had to keep checking to see if things were too much for Mara.

"We should get going," Daisy's mum said,

a few minutes later. "We don't want to wear Mara out. Daisy can come again soon."

Daisy nodded hopefully, and Mara smiled and looked as though she actually did want her to. Daisy hadn't been sure she would – they seemed to have spent half the time arguing.

On the way out of the hospital, Daisy's mum met someone she knew and stopped to chat. They went on and on talking, so Daisy wandered over to look at one of the noticeboards about fundraising. It had a few interesting photos on, but that was about it, and she was turning round to see if Mum was nearly finished when she came face to face with Jack.

"Oh. You." She said it before she thought.

"What are you doing here?" he asked.

"Visiting Mara, of course." Daisy eyed him

doubtfully. She felt like saying something snappy, even though she had seen him being so nice with Em the other day. She'd been so jealous of him, getting nuzzles from her pony.

Now that she'd been mean to him once, it seemed easier to do it again. But they were in a hospital, so he must be visiting someone who was ill. It would be really horrible of her. "Er … are you visiting someone?"

He looked surprised. "Yeah, Mara."

"*You're* visiting Mara?" Daisy stared at him. "You?"

"Why shouldn't I be?" He frowned at her as though she was being dim.

"You hate Mara!"

"No, I don't." He shrugged. "She lives almost next door to me. I see her all the time. And we go to the same riding school. I don't hate her – we just argue. She's always telling me off."

"Oh…" Daisy folded her arms across her middle. She was feeling cold again, like she had when he'd told her Em belonged to his dad.

She'd never realized Jack and Mara saw so much of each other out of school.

"I mean, I *did* see her all the time," he added. "Not for ages now." He made a weird face and Daisy suddenly realized that he was missing Mara too. It felt like she had to click everything around inside her head to make it fit again.

"Yeah…" she murmured. "I called her when I wasn't allowed to visit but it's not the same."

"Is she OK? You've just seen her…" Jack looked at her sideways. He was scared too.

"She sounded like herself – more than she did on the phone. But she does look…" Daisy caught her breath. She didn't want to say Mara looked ill. Surely she should be saying everything was brilliant? It didn't feel very loyal, saying that Mara had scared her too.

Jack's shoulders were up round his ears. "Mm. I guessed. OK. That's my mum coming," he added. "She was asking about where the ward was. See you, then."

"See you." Daisy lifted her hand awkwardly, giving him half a wave, and Jack nodded back.

7

"Daisy, hurry up! Come on, or we'll miss it!"

"I'm getting the money!" Daisy yelled back
from the kitchen. "Thanks, Mum!" She dashed
down the hallway after Oscar and grabbed
Chloe's hand. "You have to stick with me,
Mum said."

"I want a banana lolly!" Chloe told her,
tugging Daisy out of the front door. They
had lollies in the freezer but they definitely
tasted better if you'd had to race after the
ice-cream van.

"Yes, a banana lolly for you and Mum wants

a lemonade one. Oscar, is it still there? Is
it going?" Daisy called. Oscar was already
hurrying down the street.

"No, there's lots of people waiting, it's OK,"
he yelled back. "I'll go and get in the queue."

Chloe was still going on and on about the
banana lolly, so it took Daisy a little while to
notice that it was Jack in the queue in front
of them. He got a cone with two Flakes and
strawberry sauce, and Oscar was eyeing it up
enviously as he walked off.

"Can I have two Flakes?"

"No. Mum didn't give us enough money. You
can have one."

Jack stopped walking and looked back. "Oh,
hi, Daisy."

"Hi." Daisy gave him a half-smile, expecting
that he'd carry on going, but he waited for her

to buy their ice creams and then wandered
along with them.

"I'm on the way back from seeing to the
ponies," Jack explained, waving an empty
bucket at Daisy.

She nodded. "You still have to feed the little
one?"

"Yeah, but not for much longer. She's doing
well enough on her own." He slurped at his
ice cream and Oscar immediately did the
same. Daisy rolled her eyes and they both
smirked. "They're going further away now –
that's why you've been seeing them over your
way. When the foal was younger they used
to just hang around by our back gate most of
the time. They know they get carrots if they
put their heads over the gate when we're in
the garden." He took another big mouthful of

ice cream and asked, "You going to visit Mara again?" in an offhand sort of way.

"Yeah, I think Mum said we could go tomorrow. But we have to call Mara's mum first. You know, to check she's well enough."

"Yeah." He nodded and stared down at the soggy cone. They were back at Daisy's front gate by now, and Oscar and Chloe ran inside. Daisy didn't know whether to follow them or not. It felt rude to walk away from Jack but she had Mum's lemonade lolly – it was going to melt.

"Um. Do you want to come with us? To the hospital?" she asked. She didn't know why she'd done it. Maybe it was the way his shoulders were all hunched up and worried. She remembered him fussing over the ponies too... He couldn't be that bad, the way he loved them.

"Your mum wouldn't mind?" he said, looking
up hopefully. "I do want to go. It's just … the
last time I didn't know what to say. I felt bad,
like everything I was talking about was stuff
she couldn't do… Especially riding. I was
telling her about my lessons, and then Mara
went quiet and I remembered she hasn't been
on a pony for ages. So I stopped and then I
couldn't think of anything else to talk about."

Daisy nodded. "Same here. Come on. We can ask my mum now."

As she shut the front door behind them, Daisy thought how strange it was. Two weeks ago, she'd have been more likely to invite a poisonous snake inside her house than Jack Wilson.

"Do you mind it raining?" Daisy murmured to Em. It had been pouring for the last few days, which was sad as it was the last week of the summer break. Betsy had turned up her nose at a walk again, even though the rain had mostly stopped now. Mum didn't mind Daisy going to watch the ponies without Betsy as long as she had her phone and she was always back when she said she would be.

"You must be soaked. Unless ... how

waterproof are ponies? I'll have to ask Mara. Or Jack, maybe." Daisy wrinkled her nose. She wouldn't have considered giving him such a good chance to make fun of her before. What she ought to ask him was, *Why were you so mean to me?* But she didn't think she ever would. To make himself look good, she supposed. Because he had to have *someone* to pick on… She wasn't sure that being a friend of Mara's and looking after the ponies so well meant that Jack was going to be any nicer once he was back at school with his mates but maybe she wouldn't just hide behind her hair any more. She'd answered him back now – she was pretty sure she could do it again.

He hadn't teased her when they'd gone to see Mara together but it hadn't been the most successful visit. Maybe all the visitors she was getting now were tiring Mara out, Daisy thought.

She knew Kacie and Skye had been to see Mara too. This time she'd been very quiet and none of them had said much. But when they'd gone, Mara's mum had hurried out into the main part of the ward after them. She'd hugged Daisy, and then Jack, and told them they were amazing. Then she'd dashed back again, leaving them staring at each other in surprise.

Em took another mouthful of grass and looked up at Daisy. She shook her ears briskly, as if she'd made a decision, and then walked away, slow but determined, as though she knew exactly where she was going. Daisy wondered where the two chestnuts were. Perhaps the other ponies hated the rain and they'd stayed somewhere more sheltered? Em was a few metres away now, sauntering along the faint path that years and years of ponies and walkers must have worn into the turf.

Then she stopped and glanced back, peering through her fringe expectantly. As if she was telling Daisy to get a move on.

Daisy felt her mouth twist into a smile. Hurriedly, her wellies slipping a little on the soaked ground, she ran after the white pony, catching her up and standing by her shoulder. Then, without really thinking about it, she put out her hand and patted Em's neck, very gently. It was the first time that she'd touched her – that she'd touched any of the ponies. She knew she wasn't supposed to but she was sure Em had wanted her to. That look…

Em was warm, and her coat was somehow rough and silky at the same time. She gazed solemnly back at Daisy and snorted, blowing so that her damp fringe fluttered. Daisy laughed.

Slowly, she moved her hand to stroke Em's nose, running her hand over the iron-grey velvet. She held it there just for a second, as if someone was going to tell her off. Then she tucked her hands back in her pockets, grinning all over.

The pony walked on and Daisy hurried after
her. She wouldn't go far – she'd promised Mum
– but she couldn't leave Em to walk on her
own, not now. If Em went too far, she would
just turn back. She'd walked round this part
of the forest with her family and she knew the
path they were on. They were going to slope
down towards the little stream soon – she and
Oscar had spent ages there one afternoon last
summer, trying to make boats out of sticks
tied together with grass. The stream was her
boundary – she wasn't supposed to cross it
when she was out on walks with Betsy.

There wasn't so much heather here, Daisy
noticed, it was more grass and rushy plants.
It was lovely, walking slowly with a pony, she
decided. She was looking at the ground more
than she usually did when she was dashing

after Betsy. The heather was such a beautiful colour and it smelled so sweet, like honey and flowers mixed together.

Em stopped for a few mouthfuls and Daisy crouched down to look at the odd little flowers at her feet. Mum had pointed out sundew to them a while ago and she was pretty sure this was the same plant. It was a strange reddish-green, sticky-looking thing, growing low to the ground. It looked a bit like a cactus, the leaves fringed with tiny spikes, but each one was tipped with a drop of sticky dew.

Daisy peered closer, trying to see if there were any insects trapped there. The sundew plants were like Venus fly traps, Mum had said. They ate insects because the soil they lived in didn't give them enough food. She was crouched right down, looking at the sundew, when something nudged her ear. Daisy jumped and then laughed. Em was leaning down too, maybe thinking that Daisy had found something good to eat. She blew loudly in Daisy's ear.

"I don't think you'd like it," Daisy said doubtfully. "It's all sticky. But then you do like gorse and holly bushes, so what do I know?"

Em didn't eat it, though. She had a mouthful of sedge and grass instead, and walked on, picking her way carefully over the hummocky bits and avoiding the big puddles. Everything was so damp after all that rain. Daisy looked around and realized how far they'd come. It hadn't felt like it – they'd been stopping and starting and chatting and looking at flowers – but she was a good way from the patch of heathland near home.

They weren't on the path any more either, but Daisy could see it, a little way to her left, almost on top of a ridge. She and Em had wandered down a bit so they were in a flat, damp patch not far from the edge of the stream. It had been raining so much that the stream looked full, she noticed. It was roaring along a lot faster than it usually did.

"I'd better get back," Daisy said, sighing. "It must be nearly lunchtime." She pulled her phone out of her jacket pocket to check the time and made a face. Definitely lunchtime, she'd have to hurry or Mum would be getting worried about her. "Bye," she said to the white pony, who was still grazing quietly behind her. "See you soon, Em." She would have liked to stroke her again but she didn't quite dare. That one moment had been just that – a one-time thing. It felt too special to repeat.

She ought to hurry back up to the path. Daisy half turned, still looking lovingly at Em, and started to cut straight across the mossy grass. She wasn't really concentrating on where she was going. Her head was still too full of the softness of Em's nose and the silky-rough feel of her coat.

Daisy was in the mire before she knew it. Waist-deep, cold, and too shocked even to scream. She didn't understand – it had happened so quickly. She had been footsteps away from the path. How could she suddenly be up to her middle in mud? She reached out, trying to catch a tussock of grass to pull herself out. It couldn't be that difficult – she'd been on solid ground three steps before and it hadn't looked that wet...

The mud underneath her sucked and bubbled, and Daisy felt herself sinking deeper. Until then she'd been surprised and disgusted and worried about what Mum would say about her good jacket. It wasn't until she started trying to get out that she realized she might not be able to. There was nothing underneath her feet to push against. And the more she struggled, the tighter the mud seemed to suck her down.

Daisy took a deep breath, trying to keep calm. She'd try again. There was that clump of reedy grass, just *there*. She could reach it. She could.

But she couldn't.

She was stuck, completely stuck. She tried to remember the things she'd read about escaping from quicksand. That was almost the same thing, wasn't it? She'd read lots of that sort of book from the school library – the kind that told you how to punch sharks in the nose and run in zigzags away from crocodiles. Don't struggle, that was the important thing. Move slowly. She was pretty sure one of the books had said it was better to spread your weight out by lying back, rather than standing up, but she couldn't. She couldn't bear to lie down in it – she was sure she would sink under the surface. Maybe mud was different...

Don't panic and thrash about, the books all said – but Daisy could feel herself growing more panicky with every second. However hard she tried to lift her legs out, nothing happened – the mud was clinging to her too tightly.

An awful story came into her head, one that Miss Fondu had told them at school – about the mires in the forest, and how deep and dangerous they used to be. They used to swallow people up, she'd said, and not just people, whole carts and teams of horses, there one minute, gone the next. But it's not like that now, she'd explained – the drainage is much better. There were a few boggy bits still, but nothing like a couple of hundred years ago.

People did get stuck though, and ponies and cattle sometimes. She'd seen the pictures in the local paper of the fire service having to pull them out.

Ponies!

Very slowly, very carefully, Daisy turned her head to look behind her. She'd forgotten about Em in her panic. Was she stuck too?

The white pony was a couple of metres away, eyeing her worriedly as though she didn't understand what had happened. *I must have looked really strange to Em*, Daisy thought, with a gulp of panicky laughter. *There one minute, half gone the next…*

"What am I going to do?" she muttered. And then, with a worried gasp, "Don't come any nearer! Go away, Em! Please!" If the mire was deep enough to swallow Daisy up, it could trap the pony too. Was she only imagining it, or was the mud higher up her jacket than it had been? She was sinking deeper.

The white pony stood still for a moment, staring at Daisy – and then she stepped delicately forward. Daisy watched her in horror, shaking her head. "No, no, no… Em, don't. Please!"

But the pony seemed to know exactly where she was going. She placed her hooves so carefully, as though she could tell where the solid ground was. That was what had happened, Daisy realized. She had been walking with Em before. The pony had followed her own safe path through the mire, something she probably did all the time, and Daisy had been right next to her every step of the way. But on her way back Daisy had cut across the mossy grass to the path – the mossy grass that had been hiding the bog.

Em came closer, very slowly, but then about a metre away from Daisy she stopped and lowered her head as if she was sniffing out the boggy ground. She stopped, stepping from foot to foot uncomfortably like she wanted to come closer but knew she couldn't.

"Don't," Daisy whispered. "Stay there."

Daisy looked down, her heart suddenly hammering in relief as she remembered. "Oh! My phone!" She could call Mum. She reached her right hand towards her jacket pocket and then she let out a little whimpering sound. Her pockets were full of mud – they were well beneath the wet, slimy surface. Her phone must be soaked. Mum was probably calling her this minute, Daisy thought, and she pressed her muddy hand against her mouth, trying not to howl.

Then she took a deep breath and yelled instead, as loud as she could. "Help! Please! I'm stuck! Help! Help!"

There was a startled twittering as a bird launched itself into the air from a bush a few metres away but no helpful walker called back to her, no one came running. She tried calling again and then again. A pause for breath and then more shouting. Her throat was hurting.

Still nothing.

Faint hoofbeats sounded behind her and Daisy craned over her shoulder again. Em was walking off. *That's good*, Daisy told herself. Em needed to get out of danger – it was the right thing to do. But seeing the white pony walk steadily away from her was heart-breaking. It felt as if she was being abandoned forever. She wanted to scream to Em to come back, come back please…

Instead she called, "Help!" again but she could tell her voice was softer already. The mud was up to the fifth button on her jacket now.

Time seemed to pass so much more slowly
after Em had left her. Daisy had no idea how
long she'd been trapped. She went on trying
to shout but it was hopeless. There was no one
there to shout to.

She was so cold she couldn't feel her feet any
more, except for a weird, horrible squeezing.
She was feeling cold inside too, and more and
more frightened. What if no one ever came
close enough to hear her shouting? Or what if
they did, but it was the five minutes that Daisy
was too tired and cold and scared to bother

calling out? She thought of that and then spent the next few minutes shouting, "Help! Help!" until her voice was nearly gone.

There was nothing she could do – that was what was so awful. She was helpless. After a while, the thought came to her – was this what Mara felt like? Stuck, with nothing she could do to make herself better? She started shivering, her teeth chattering, and she wasn't sure if it was because she was cold, or terrified, or both…

"You idiot! How did you end up in there?"

Daisy yelped. She only realized as she jerked awake that she'd almost been asleep, worn out with shouting and struggling and the awful clinging heaviness of the mud. She must have been in there for an hour at least. Maybe longer.

She floundered, flapping her arms out of the
mud and making a sort of strangled gulping
sound as she slid in a little deeper.

She stared at Jack and Em, standing on the
path a few metres away from her. She'd never
seen Jack look so angry – but then looking at
the scarlet patches on his cheeks, she saw it
was mostly because he was scared.

"You never go near the bogs, never! What do you think those signs about keeping to the path mean?"

"It was an accident," she whispered hoarsely. "I didn't mean to."

"Good," he muttered, looking around as if he was hoping someone else would come along to help.

"How did you know I was here?" she coughed.

"Snowball, of course. Keep still, don't flap about. I'm going to see if I can find a stick to pull you out with." He ran off. Panicked, Daisy tried to stretch up her head to watch for him coming back but she was too cold and tired to move.

"I said don't flap! You'll sink more. I couldn't find anything long enough for you to hold on to but I can test the ground with this." He poked at the mossy patches between them and stepped forwards. Em came with him, setting each foot down with the greatest of care.

"What did you mean about Em?" Daisy asked.

"The pony? She came and got me. She just kept circling in front of the gate. Uuugh!" He jumped back as the stick sank right in. "Not that way, then. Don't you have a phone?" he added crossly.

"It's all wet in my pocket," Daisy whispered. She didn't care if he thought she was useless right now.

"It's going to be OK," he muttered. "I'll get you out. Or if I can't, I'll run home and call nine-nine-nine." He stepped forwards cautiously and gave a relieved sigh as the ground under him held. "I thought maybe one of the other ponies was hurt. Mum's at work and Dad's out checking on the cows, so I thought I'd better see what was wrong. And I didn't think of bringing my phone, which was stupid. Not as stupid as you falling in a bog, though!"

"Thanks for following her," Daisy whispered. "She's amazing. She's like one of those hero dogs that saves people."

"Yeah. Hey, look, can you reach the stick now? If you stretch?"

Daisy reached out. Her arms felt like bits of stone, heavy and lifeless. She wasn't sure she'd be able to grip on to anything, even if she could reach.

"A bit more," Jack coaxed. "Come on!" Then he sighed. "No? OK. Wait a minute. Hey, careful!" That was to Em, who was nudging him. "You'll have me in it too." But then he looked consideringly at the pony for a moment and grabbed hold of a chunk of her white mane.

"I'm not sure how long she's going to let me do this," he called to Daisy, stepping forward and leaning right out over the treacherous bright moss. "Especially when we start pulling. We'd better be fast. Grab on!"

Daisy heaved herself forwards with one last

desperate effort and caught the stick in both hands. It was amazing the difference it made, having something to pull against. She could make her feet move! She felt the mud easing its grip with a dreadful sucking sound, and then she was half stumbling, half crawling out of the mire and falling against Em and Jack.

"You look disgusting. Like some sort of swamp monster. Ugh, and you smell. You're getting it all over me – yuck!"

Daisy didn't care. She almost wanted to hug him. She *did* stagger up and hug Em, until she realized she was leaving more mud on the pony's white coat. "Oh, sorry…" she said, trying to brush it off, but she was only making it worse. Em stood solidly, letting Daisy lean against her.

"It doesn't matter," Jack said. "I'll brush it off for her." Then he looked at Daisy worriedly. "Are you crying?"

"No…" She was, actually, but she wasn't sure why. It was silly to be crying *now*, when everything was OK.

"You'd better keep holding on to her," Jack suggested. "She won't mind. I'd say ride her

back home but she's never been broken for
riding. Put your arm round her neck." He
tutted as Daisy just stood
there and grabbed her arm,
putting it round Em's
neck for her. "There.
Come on, good girl."
He clicked his tongue,
coaxing Em on, but
Daisy didn't think
he was making much
difference. Em was
walking anyway, slowly,
surely, letting Daisy
stumble along beside her.

They were on the heathland, about to take
the path through the trees to the back of
Daisy's house when her dad found them.

He came racing
out of the trees
and grabbed
her, swinging
her up and
hugging her so
tight she yelped.
"What
happened? Where
have you been?
Daisy, we were
so worried!" He
shifted her round
so she was sitting
on his hip, like he
did with Chloe, and Daisy laid her head on
his shoulder. She was just too tired to explain.
"Look at the state of you…"

"She stepped in one of the boggy patches," Jack said. He was looking a bit nervous, as if he thought Daisy's dad was going to tell him off.

"Jack and Em rescued me," she muttered wearily. "Em's the pony. She went and got Jack. Oh, Dad… My phone got wet in the bog. I'm really sorry."

"Oh wow." Dad shook his head. "Wow, Daisy. You're not supposed to go beyond the stream without someone with you. We should ncver have let you go out on your own."

"I didn't … I was just next to the stream… Why aren't you at work?" Daisy said, suddenly looking up.

"Because Mum called me in a panic when you didn't turn up for lunch and you weren't answering your phone! I was on my way back to the house to tell her we had to call the police!"

"Oh…" Daisy tried to wriggle away and stand up but he wouldn't let her go.

"Sorry… Sorry, I didn't mean to shout. I was scared. I am scared, now, thinking about it."

"I'll pay for a new phone myself out of my pocket money," Daisy said hesitantly.

"I don't care about the phone." Her dad rested his chin on her hair for a moment. Then he looked back at Jack. "Do your parents know where you are?"

"Um, not exactly. My dad was out with his cows. I left him a note on the table saying I was going to check on Snowball. That's what we call her," he explained, nodding at Em. "She belongs to my dad. Em's Daisy's name for her."

Daisy sighed into her dad's sleeve. She still thought Em was better.

"OK. Look, you'd better come home with us,

have a hot drink, and we can call your dad and let him know everything's OK. Come on." He set Daisy down on her feet again but he was holding on to her, his arm wrapped tightly round her shoulders.

Jack started to follow but Em stayed by the first of the trees. She gazed after them for a moment, then she lowered her head and started to graze.

"She's not coming?" Daisy sighed.

"I'll find her later and brush the mud off her," Jack said. "I can bring her a treat. Some apples maybe."

"She deserves more than apples," Dad said, and Daisy nodded. She watched Em as they walked away, quietly eating the grass, as if she didn't think she'd done anything all that special.

There was a disbelieving sort of silence on the other end of the phone, and then Mara said, "You actually fell right in? All the way? Not just lost a welly kind of falling in the bog?"

"Yup. Up to my waist. And then I sank further in. I did lose a welly too. But my feet were so cold I couldn't feel them by the time I got out. I didn't notice till I got home!"

"But how did you get out? You didn't have
to call the fire brigade, did you?" Mara asked.
She was starting to sound worried now. "I put
a foot in once and it was awful."

"Jack and Em pulled me out."

"No! You're not serious?" Mara squealed.
"Jack rescued you?"

"It was more Em really. She went and fetched
him – she was amazing! She's the cleverest
pony ever."

"Hang on, you mean Jack wasn't with you to
start with?"

"No," Daisy explained patiently, and she
began the story again, with Mara interrupting
every other sentence. Daisy felt like she'd
told loads of people about it now – Dad,
Mum, Jack's dad when he came to pick
Jack up, Chloe and Oscar about six times…

Even Betsy seemed to have worked out that
something had happened. The little dog
was snuggled up against Daisy now, looking
watchful. "She went to his back gate and she
made him follow her."

"It's like a film," Mara said, with a shocked
sort of whistle. "Are you OK?"

"Yeah … but I've had three showers and it
still feels like there's mud all over me."

Mara snorted and Daisy started to laugh too.
She hadn't heard Mara make that noise in so
long. Her proper laughing snort – the noise she
made when something was really, really funny.

"Yeah, well, glad I cheered you up…"

"You've got to admit it is a bit funny!"
Mara was silent for a moment. "Apart from
what might have happened if Em hadn't been
so clever."

"I know," Daisy whispered. "But … someone would have walked past. After a while." She shivered, remembering how it had felt, being all alone in the mire.

"Maybe. You were so lucky."

Daisy gripped the phone a little tighter. "Yeah. I know."

9

Mara was still in hospital when Daisy went
back to school in September and Daisy didn't
know when she'd be coming out. Her mum was
starting to look more quietly hopeful, though.
The last time Daisy had been to visit Mara,
she'd just come back from the hospital school.
She was strong enough to go there most days
now. She'd spent most of Daisy's visit moaning
about it but Daisy thought that secretly Mara
was glad to have something to do.

Daisy had actually been looking forward
to school for a change. Mum and Dad had

gone into an enormous panic about her being caught in the mire, which she supposed was fair enough. It could have been a lot worse – she tried not to think about what might have happened. But it seemed that Mum couldn't stop thinking about it.

Daisy wasn't allowed out in the forest on her own any more. Not even to walk Betsy. She'd tried to argue about that and Mum had got so angry she really shouted, which she hardly ever did. Half the time it felt completely unfair and then she remembered that cold feeling inside, when she'd thought that no one was going to find her. Then she almost wished that Mum and Dad would never let her go out again.

Daisy was hoping that they'd change their minds eventually but for the last week of the holidays she'd had to take Betsy for walks

with Mum or Dad, or Mum and Dad and
Oscar and Chloe... It wasn't the same. She'd
seen Em and the two other ponies out on
the heath but there was no way to get close
to them with her brother and sister charging
about. She hadn't been able to get near
enough to say what she wanted to say. *Thank
you for rescuing me. I love you. I always knew
you were special.* She had stood watching Em
from a distance, thinking it as hard as she
could and hoping Em knew.

It was good to get to school on the first day
and find out that she'd been made one of the
House Captains. All the others – Jack was one
of them – were loud, confident sorts of people.
Mara would have been a House Captain, of
course. Daisy wanted to ask the head, Ms
Davies, why they'd chosen her but she didn't.

What if Ms Davies suddenly realized what a silly mistake they'd made? Daisy just hoped that Ms Davies never heard about her falling in a bog and having to be rescued by a pony.

Jack had told his mates about it and everyone kept asking her what it had been like, being stuck. For once, Jack had managed to make Daisy sound interesting. He'd told them that Em – except he said Snowball – had done most of the rescuing. It was quite cool to be rescued by a pony.

The new House Captains had to stand up at the front in assembly, with all the Juniors looking at them, and Daisy was surprised to find she actually enjoyed it. Even Oscar seemed impressed with his big sister and didn't pull faces for once. Daisy was looking forward to telling Mum at the end of the day –

although if she wasn't quick Oscar would break the news first, she realized as she went to fetch her new jacket from the cloakroom. She should have hurried. Oh well.

"Hey, Daisy!"

Daisy looked over the coat racks and found Jack grabbing his stuff too. "Oh, hi." She rolled her eyes. "Thanks for telling everyone about me getting covered in mud…"

"I didn't say it like that!" Jack looked indignant.

Daisy grinned. "I know. I was only joking." Then she looked at him thoughtfully. "You would have done, before. You'd have been mean about it."

Jack shrugged uncomfortably. "Yeah. I know. I'm sorry. I was mean to you…"

Daisy waited for him to explain why but he didn't. She wasn't sure he even knew.

"I liked it that you said Em cared enough
about me to want to get me out," she said
at last. She sighed. "I really miss her."

"So where have you been?" Jack asked. "I looked for you out on the heath."

"Guess."

"You're grounded?"

"Sort of. Not allowed out by myself ever, ever again. That's what my mum says." Daisy sighed. She'd forgotten, almost, in her excitement at being made House Captain.

"Good!" Jack smirked.

"Hey!"

Jack shrugged. "Maybe it is a bit unfair. You probably wouldn't fall in a bog again."

"Never." Daisy shuddered. Then she picked up her backpack. "I've got to go. Mum'll be waiting."

"You're not even allowed to walk home from school?"

"I wouldn't be anyway – Oscar, remember?

Mum wouldn't let me walk Oscar back – he never listens to me."

They walked out of the cloakroom and down the corridor. Just as they were getting to the main doors, Jack said thoughtfully, "What about if you were with me?"

Daisy stopped, blinking in surprise. She moved out of the way of the door so a couple of Year Fours could get past. "What, would they let me go out? I don't know. Would you – I mean – would you want to?"

"Snowball likes you." Jack shrugged. "I know she's a free-roaming pony. She's meant to be wild. But they do recognize some people. I reckon she's been looking for you."

"Really?" Daisy was so pleased her voice squeaked. Too pleased even to be annoyed about Jack using Em's real name.

"Yeah. I could ask your mum, if you like."

"You can try…" Daisy said doubtfully. "Hopefully she'll be pleased about me being a House Captain. She might say yes."

"Oh, yeah, well done."

"You too." Daisy was silent for a moment. "Do you think they only made me House Captain because Mara's not here?"

Jack stared at her. "What would they do that for?"

"I don't know." Daisy shrugged. "I mean… I'm not one of those people."

"You're really clever, and you do the library club with Mr Williams, and last term you made everyone save their crisp packets so you could send them to that recycling thing. And everyone knows you're still visiting Mara. You put those photos of her up on the class

noticeboard and the letters from her. All the
Year Ones want you to play with them. You're
the nice one." He folded his arms. "Want me
to keep telling you all this stuff?"

"Er … no," Daisy muttered. She could feel
her face getting red. "Mum's going to be
wondering where I am."

"Your mum likes me," Jack pointed out,
looking smug. "She thinks I rescued you, even
though it was mostly Snowball. Come on, I bet
I can get her to change her mind."

Mum was looking slightly worried by the
time they got across the playground – although
they weren't even the last ones out. She was
going to keep on being like that for ages, Daisy
thought. It didn't bode well for Jack's plan.

"Oh, there you are, Daisy! Oscar told me your
news. Well done! And you're a House Captain

as well, aren't you?" She beamed at Jack.

"Yes. Um. Mrs Hamilton?"

"It's fine to call me Laura," Daisy's mum
said, still smiling at Jack. *She really does think he
rescued me all by himself*, Daisy realized. *Maybe
she is going to say yes…*

Jack nodded. "I was wondering … would it be OK for Daisy to come out to see Snowball with me sometime, please?"

Oscar started to make a whistling noise and Daisy elbowed him. Luckily Mum was still looking at Jack, as well as trying to keep an eye on Chloe climbing the playground fence.

"Snowball? The pony – the one that Daisy was with…?"

Daisy could see Mum starting to shake her head but Jack wasn't giving up.

"Yes, my dad's pony. She came and found me when Daisy was stuck. I think she misses Daisy."

"Why would she miss Daisy?" Mum looked confused.

"I used to see her loads when I was walking Betsy," Daisy explained. "I always looked out

for her. I'd be careful, Mum, I promise. We'd
stay together and I'd keep away from the
stream – I'd just stay on the heath. Even if
Em – I mean Snowball – went further off,
I wouldn't."

"Perhaps after school tomorrow?" Jack
suggested. "I could walk back with you."
He looked hopefully at Daisy's mum. Daisy
could tell she wanted to say no but she
was torn. After all, Jack was the one who'd
brought Daisy back. And she knew Mum
had been worrying about her feeling lonely
at school...

"Maybe for a little while," she murmured
doubtfully, and Jack nodded.

"OK. See you tomorrow, Daisy! Bye!"

Daisy watched him go. She wanted to jump
up and down and punch the air but she didn't

want to make Mum think too hard about what she'd said yes to.

"Do you think it's OK to tell Mara about being a House Captain?" she asked Mum, partly to distract her and partly because she actually wanted to know. "Because if she'd been at school I bet it would have been her. What if she's upset?"

Mum reached out to give her a hug. "You mustn't let thinking that spoil it for you, Daisy-petal. I don't think that's true anyway. You'd both have been captains."

They wouldn't, because they were in the same house and it was always one girl and one boy for each, but Daisy decided not to bother explaining.

"It's tricky, though," Mum went on. "I think Mara would be pleased for you. But it must be

so hard for her, knowing she's missing out...
Maybe only tell her if she asks?"

"Yeah. You're right." Daisy sighed. "I can tell
her about going to see Em with Jack instead,"
she added cleverly, and Mum didn't say no...

"She's so beautiful," Daisy said happily. They
had Betsy with them, so she couldn't get too
close but she could see that Em was plump and
her coat was shiny. The flaxen chestnut mare
and her foal Acorn were close by too – the foal
was definitely getting bigger.

Jack nodded. "I know." He frowned
thoughtfully at Em and then looked back at
Daisy. "Do you think she's in foal?"

"What, you mean she's having a baby?"
Daisy yelped.

Jack rolled his eyes. "Yes. She could be. There was a stallion running with the mares here back in May. Don't you remember? There were signs up telling everyone to stay out of the way. The ponies get a bit wild and go dashing all over the place."

"Oh … yes, I think so." Daisy nodded. She did remember Dad saying to be careful, now she thought about it. "How can you tell she's in foal? I can't see any difference."

"I don't know either, not for sure, but she does look a bit fatter. Ponies don't really show until about six months. That would be…" He was obviously counting in his head. "November. It could just be that she's been feeding up over the summer. That would be fine too. We want them in good condition if they're staying on the forest over the winter."

Daisy nodded, trying to look knowledgeable, but she had a feeling that Jack liked showing off a bit.

"Do you want me to ask my dad if you can come and watch the drift at the end of October?" Jack called back as he went to look at Bracken.

Daisy nodded excitedly. "Yes! Yes, please. But I thought we weren't allowed? Dad wanted to take us to see it last autumn but someone at work told him we shouldn't go because it's dangerous."

Her dad had been quite disappointed, she remembered. He'd heard about the drift before they moved to the New Forest. Traditionally the ponies were rounded up every year to be checked over and registered, and to have their tails marked — this had been going on for hundreds of years, since the 1500s. But too many people had been getting in the way, and the verderers – the old name for the officials who looked after the forest – had said it wasn't safe for people to go and watch any more.

"Yeah, my dad rides out to help round up the ponies but I'm not old enough. We can watch from our paddock, though. It's not far from where they set up the pound for the ponies and you always get to see some of them being driven past. We can take sandwiches and sit on the fence."

"That would be brilliant." Daisy nodded happily. She might not mention sitting on the fence to Mum and Dad, she decided. Not the way they were currently feeling. She'd say they would absolutely definitely be behind the fence the whole time.

"There's my dad!" Jack elbowed Daisy and pointed at one of the riders speeding towards them. Daisy couldn't see much more than a tall man in a riding helmet on a black pony but she waved all the same, and Jack's dad just about waved. He was concentrating on not letting the ponies he was herding double back and he only glanced their way for a moment.

"Was he wearing a thing like a life jacket?" Daisy asked, after the little gang of ponies had thundered past. "Your dad, I mean. He had a sort of padded vest on."

"It's a special one." Jack nodded. "It inflates if you fall off. Before you even hit the ground. Lots of people have accidents riding for the drift – you're twisting and turning so much, it's easy to have a fall. Last year he got knocked off when he went under a tree and got hit by a low branch. Mum was cross and said he wasn't being careful enough. The vest's supposed to protect your back, so you don't hurt your spine or break your ribs if you fall."

"That's clever," Daisy said, and then she added, "I went to see Mara after school yesterday." Broken ribs had made her think of hospitals. "She was really jealous that we were getting to see the drift. She said next year she's definitely coming too."

She and Jack exchanged a glance, and Jack nodded. "She will," he said firmly.

Daisy glanced away. "Oh, look, there's more coming! Hey, is that Em? Snowball, I mean?" She was still trying to remember to call Em by her right name around Jack. She hadn't told

162

him why she called the white pony Em. She
hadn't told anyone.

Jack leaned out to look. "Yes! And the other
two. Good, they don't look too stressed. It's
Acorn's first time being rounded up but she's
just going with the others."

The three ponies were with a group of
about ten and there were four riders herding
them along the path past the fence. Daisy
felt herself shrinking back a little. The path
wasn't that close but the ponies were going so
fast, she could almost feel the wind and dust
as they galloped by. She fixed her eyes on
Em, white mane flying, her tail flowing out
behind her as she whirled past. Bracken and
Acorn were just behind her – they were gone
in seconds.

"Wow…" Daisy whispered.

Jack laughed. "Told you it was fun."

"Yeah – but is Em OK, going that fast? If she's having a foal?"

"She'll be fine."

"Is your dad going to bring her into the paddock to look after her?" Daisy asked, climbing down from the fence to get the biscuits Mum had given her.

"No. Not unless she starts to look as though there's something wrong. She'll most likely have her foal out here."

Daisy pulled a face. "I suppose that's OK. It just seems like she should be in hospital or something, you know? Don't laugh at me!"

"We'll look out for her, we always do! Me or Dad, we keep an eye on them. But she's not going to have the foal until April at least."

"April? That's ages away." Daisy sighed.

"Same time the new grass is growing," Jack pointed out. "So they can eat loads and feed the foals properly."

Daisy nodded. It still seemed such a long time – by April, everything could be different.

10

The loud banging on the side door startled
Daisy and Chloe dropped her spoon in her
cereal, splashing milk everywhere. Then the
door rattled and swung open, and Jack looked
round it, scarlet-faced and panting.

"Go out to the heath!" he yelled. "Not far
off the two trees. Go on, I've got to go and
get my dad!" Then he shot out of the door,
pulling it shut behind him with a slam.
Betsy popped out from under the table and
barked excitedly – clearly she could tell that
something was happening.

"What was … what was that all about?"
Mum said, staring at the space where Jack had
been. "Daisy, do you know?"

"No… Oh! Maybe! Mum, can I go, please
please please?"

"Not until you tell me what's going on – and
what did he mean, the two trees?"

"The two joined together, the oak tree and
the beech tree, you know. Dad showed me! I
told you about it! And I'm not sure but I think
Em might have had her foal – that's why Jack's
gone to get his dad."

"Can we go and see?" Oscar jumped up
hopefully and Chloe followed him.

Daisy bit her lip. She was desperate to see
Em and the newborn foal but Em wasn't going
to want loads of people around.

"Maybe later," Mum said firmly. "Daisy, you

can go. But you have to be back in an hour. If there's anything wrong, if you need me to call a vet for you, let me know."

"I will! Thanks, Mum!" Daisy was already hopping about trying to get her wellies on, ignoring Oscar trying to argue and Chloe thumping the table. The foal – it had to be, she couldn't think why else Jack would be so excited.

She sped down the side of the house and out to the pathway. The two trees that Jack had mentioned grew at the edge of the heath, a few hundred metres from the path they always took through the patch of woodland. It wasn't on one of the main paths and it was a little quieter. It made sense that Em would want to have her baby there, out of everyone's way.

As she came closer, Daisy slowed to a walk,

watching out for a flash of white coat, but
it was Bracken she saw first, standing guard
with Acorn at the edge of the heath. The two
chestnuts turned to gaze at Daisy and she
stopped, wondering if they didn't want her to
come any closer. She couldn't see Em – then
there was a little movement behind the clump
of gorse bushes.

Daisy stood on tiptoe, trying to peer over the bright gorse flowers, but she still couldn't really see. Bracken moved, swishing her tail, and Daisy wondered whether the chestnut pony was trying to shoo her away. But instead Bracken wandered out on to the open grassland and Acorn followed her. The two of them began to graze. They weren't worried about her, Daisy realized, with a little glow of pleasure. They didn't mind her going to look at the foal.

Slowly, she crept round the bushes – the flaring yellow flowers smelled of coconut and the scent always made her happy. Em was standing on the other side of the gorse, head down, nosing at something on the ground. She swung her head round at Daisy, ears pricking right forward, and her nostrils flared. Then she seemed to realize who it was, and relaxed.

"Hey," Daisy whispered. "I can go, if you like…" She wanted to see the foal, of course, but not if Em was scared – or if she just wanted some time on her own with her baby.

Em made a noise Daisy hadn't heard before, a soft, throaty sort of noise, and stepped a little sideways. Behind her, tucked safely up against the gorse bushes, was a white foal. It was lying on the ground and it seemed to have legs everywhere, much too long for its body.

Daisy heard running footsteps behind her and she hurried out to wave at Jack. "She's here!" she whispered. "And the foal. It's not standing up, though. I hope it's OK."

"She's had it? That was quick! She was just starting when I saw her. Let's see." He craned round the edge of the bushes, just as Daisy had. "Another grey!"

"Does it matter that the foal's not standing up?" Daisy asked anxiously, but Jack shook his head.

"I don't think so. I've only seen one other really new foal like this and it took him a while to stand up too. We should just stay back and watch."

They stood at the edge of the gorse bushes, watching Em nudge gently at her baby. At last the foal decided to try standing up but its legs were so long and gangly that it didn't seem to know quite what to do with them. They stuck out all over the place. At one point the foal was sitting on its back legs like a dog, staring down at its front legs in pure confusion. Then, at last, it managed to wobble on to all four hooves – more by accident than anything else. It stood there looking dopey for a moment, while Em licked at it, cleaning up its sticky coat.

"Em looks really pleased with herself," Daisy whispered to Jack. "I wish Mara was here to see the foal too. She'd be so excited."

"I know," Jack breathed. "Hang on, I'll take a photo for her. Ah, look, it's trying to feed."

The foal staggered round to Em's side, still
wobbly, and nosed at her stomach with a strange
little squeaky neigh. It was clearly trying to
find her teats. It took a while but at last the
foal worked it out, and sucked gratefully for a
minute or two. Then it decided it needed a rest
and tried to lie down, bending its knees. But its
legs seemed to wobble in different directions,
so it straightened them out again, peering at
the ground as if it wasn't sure why that hadn't
worked.

It tried again, and then gave up and just
slumped, squashing the gawky legs up
underneath its body. Then it lay there, dozing,
folded up into a leggy, magical little parcel.

Em stood watching, ever so often lowering
her head to look more closely. She glanced
round again to check on Jack and Daisy, and

then went back to admiring her baby. Daisy
thought she'd never seen a pony look so
proud of herself.

"You will be careful, won't you?" Daisy's mum whispered to her as the two girls pulled on their coats.

"Yes! Mum, shh! She'll hear you."

"OK, OK. But Mara's only just out of hospital, Daisy. You have to be so careful."

Daisy rolled her eyes and followed Mara out to the garden gate.

"Was that your mum telling you not to let anything happen to me?" Mara asked, pulling her bandana tighter. Her hair was starting to grow back but it was still only wispy.

"Sorry." Daisy gave her an apologetic look. "Is it driving you mad?"

"A bit. I had to promise my mum I'd go home and not move for the rest of the day if she let me come with you."

"Jack knows exactly where they are – he called me just before you got here. It won't take us five minutes to find them," Daisy promised. "He said he was sure they wouldn't go far."

"I can't wait." Mara did look as though she was desperate to race away into the woods, Daisy thought. She was bouncing on her toes.

They'd been planning this together ever since Mara had rung her up a few days earlier, so excited she could hardly speak. It had taken her ages to make Daisy understand what she was saying – that she was allowed out of hospital. She wasn't completely better – the doctors wouldn't be able to say that definitely for a long time – but she was in remission. She could even go back to school if things went well. She'd be there for the

summer term, their last term. She'd be able
to start at the secondary school with everyone
else in September.

The path looked almost like something from
a fairy tale today, Daisy thought. The trees
were just opening out into full leaf now, the
greens acid-bright, and there was a little patch
of white wood anemones that the ponies and
deer hadn't found yet. They were like stars,
shining in their dark leaves.

It was pure good luck that Em and
Snowdrop and the others were so close today.
For the past week they'd been further over by
the mire and there was no way Mara could
walk that far yet. Anyway, Daisy had avoided
that part of the forest ever since last summer.
Even on the brightest, sunniest days, it still
felt strange and chilly.

"Oh, I can see them!" Mara whispered. "That's her, isn't it?"

Daisy nodded. "Yes." She gazed proudly at the four ponies – posed so beautifully under a huge tree with a clump of bluebells nearby. The flowers made Em and Snowdrop look even whiter than usual. It was as if they'd found the perfect spot to show themselves off to Mara for the first time.

"She's so pretty – they both are," Mara murmured. "Snowdrop looks so big – I can't believe she's only a week old."

Daisy nodded. "She's doing really well, Jack's dad says. She's strong." She glanced sideways at Mara. She'd never actually spoken to her about how important the pony had been for her during that worst part of the year, when she'd been so unhappy about school. She'd been

frightened of talking to Mara about anything
back then.

"It's strange, her arriving just now, isn't it?"
Daisy said quietly, looking back at the white
foal. Snowdrop kept setting off on wild little
runs, kicking up her legs and darting about.
She circled back to Em every couple of
minutes, though, making sure that her mum
was just where she'd left her.

Mara was silent but Daisy could *feel* her
listening, thinking.

"You mean, now I'm out of hospital?" she
said at last.

"Yeah…" Daisy said, uncomfortably. "Does
that sound funny? It's like – new things are
happening. Back in the summer, when you
hadn't been in hospital that long, I used to
come out here and watch Em. That was before

I knew she belonged to Jack's family."

"I know you did! You sent me all those photos
of her. And the drawing. It was such a good
picture – I can see how much it's like her!"

"Yeah. I didn't tell you everything, though.
She was – I was almost sure that seeing her
helped. Because you loved seeing her photos
and talking about her, I started feeling as if Em
was helping you get well." Daisy shrugged. "It
sounds weird."

"It isn't weird." Mara smiled. She looked
tired, Daisy thought, wondering if they ought
to go back. Tired, but happy. "You sending
me stuff made me feel as if I was still there.
And you kept calling and telling me about her,
even when I was so tired all I did was sigh at
you… You hadn't forgotten about me. Em's our
pony angel."

"Yes!" Daisy looked at Em, cropping grass and keeping one eye on her bouncy foal. Her long white fringe was in her eyes again but the sun was on her coat and she almost glowed against the bluebells. "That's it. She was exactly what you needed."

"And you were the one who found her for me," Mara pointed out.

"Yeah." Daisy came to stand by the tree next to her best friend, and they watched the white foal dancing around her mum. Em lifted her head to look back at them, her ears flicking back and forth in the sunlight. "Yes, I suppose I did."

*Get your paws on
the brand-new series
from Holly Webb —
out now!*

International best-selling author

HOLLY WEBB

Museum Kittens

The Midnight Visitor

Illustrated by Sarah Lodge

HOLLY WEBB

Holly Webb started out as a children's book editor and wrote her first series for the publisher she worked for. She has been writing ever since, with over one hundred books to her name. Holly lives in Berkshire, with her husband and three children. Holly's pet cats are always nosying around when she is trying to type on her laptop.

For more information
about Holly Webb visit:

www.holly-webb.com